nickelodeon

SpongeBob SQUAREPANTS

READY, SET, GO!

Based on the TV series *SpongeBob SquarePants*™ created by Stephen Hillenburg
as seen on Nickelodeon™

Ready-to-Read

SIMON SPOTLIGHT/NICKELODEON
An imprint of Simon & Schuster Children's Publishing Division
New York   London   Toronto   Sydney
1230 Avenue of the Americas, New York, New York 10020
Camp SpongeBob © 2004 Viacom International Inc.
The Big Win © 2008 Viacom International Inc.
For information about special discounts for bulk purchases, please contact
Simon & Schuster Special Sales at 1-866-506-1949 or business@simonandschuster.com.
Manufactured in the United States of America 0311 LAK
This Simon Spotlight edition 2011
2 4 6 8 10 9 7 5 3 1
ISBN 978-1-4424-1341-2
These titles were previously published individually by Simon Spotlight.

CAMP SPONGEBOB

by Molly Reisner and Kim Ostrow
illustrated by Heather Martinez

It was a perfect summer day
in Bikini Bottom. Sandy spent
the morning practicing her
new karate moves.
"Hiiiyaaaa! All this sunshine
makes me more energetic
than a jackrabbit after a cup
of coffee," she said.

"Hey, Sandy, where did you first
learn karate anyway?"
SpongeBob asked.
Sandy told her friend about her days
at Master Kim's Karate Camp.

". . . and I won the championship!"
Sandy finished breathlessly.
SpongeBob leaped in the air.
"Camp sounds amazing!" he shouted.
"But I never got to go."

"When I was little, my dream
was to go to camp. But every summer
my parents sent me to Grandma's.
Sometimes I would pretend she was
my counselor, but I am not sure she
was cut out for camp life,"
SpongeBob said, sighing.

"Say no more, SpongeBob,"
  said Sandy. "Let's open Bikini
  Bottom's first summer camp.
  You can be my assistant."
"I can?" asked SpongeBob.
"Yes, and we can get started
  today," said Sandy.
"I am ready!" shouted SpongeBob.

Sandy gathered Squidward and
Patrick to tell them about the camp.
"Oh, please," Squidward said,
moaning. "Camp is for children."
"Exactly!" shouted SpongeBob.
"It would be for all the little
children of Bikini Bottom."

"Hmmm," Squidward thought out loud.
"Perhaps I could teach the
kids around here a thing or two.
Everyone would look up to me."

"That sounds like lots of fun," said Patrick. "When I was at starfish camp, we used to lie around in the sun and sleep a lot. I could teach everyone how to do that!"

"I will teach karate!"
declared Sandy, kicking the air.

"Now go on home and practice what you are going to teach. Let's meet back here tomorrow," said Sandy.

The next day SpongeBob woke up
in the best mood ever.
"To be a good assistant, I need
to make sure I am prepared
with good camper activities,"
he told Gary.
SpongeBob thought of making Krabby
Patties and having bubble-blowing
contests. He imagined whole days
spent jellyfishing.

SpongeBob ran around his house
gathering all the items he needed.
"Whistle! Check. Megaphone! Check.
Visor! Check. Clipboard?"
Gary slithered over
to SpongeBob's bed and meowed.
"Good job, Gary! Check!"

SpongeBob went over to the mirror and raised his arms. "Camping assistants need to be strong!" he reminded himself as he flexed his muscles. "Now I am ready!"

SpongeBob ran over
to the treedome.
Sandy was chopping
wood with her bare hands.
"SpongeBob SquarePants reporting
for duty!" he said, blowing his
whistle three times.

"As a good assistant, I request permission to check on everyone to make sure they are practicing their duties."

"Go for it, SpongeBob," said Sandy.

First SpongeBob went to
Patrick's rock. He watched quietly
as Patrick practiced the art of sleeping.
Then SpongeBob blew his whistle.
Patrick jumped up.
"Just making sure you are working
 hard," explained SpongeBob.
"Now go back to sleep!"

Next SpongeBob peeked
inside Squidward's house.
"I can't hear you,"
sang SpongeBob.
"Practice makes perfect."

SpongeBob went back to see Sandy,
who was working on her karate moves.
"All counselors are working hard,"
reported SpongeBob.
"Now what should I do?"

"Take a load off and have some
lemonade," suggested Sandy.
"No time for lemonade,"
said SpongeBob.
"As your assistant, I am here
to assist. How can I assist?"

23

"Listen, little buddy," said Sandy.
"You are acting nuttier than a bag
of walnuts at the county fair.
This camp is supposed to be fun."
"I will make sure it is fun!
With my assistance, this will
be the best camp ever!"
SpongeBob said, cheering.

"Attention, counselors, please
report to me right away,"
SpongeBob said. They all ran to him.
"Now go back to your posts and
PRACTICE! Camp opens tomorrow."

That night SpongeBob was
so excited, he could not sleep.
He decided to visit all the
counselors just to make sure
they were ready.

"Squidward," he whispered.
Squidward was fast asleep.
SpongeBob blew his whistle.
"Just making sure you are all
set for tomorrow."
"You are killing me, SpongeBob,"
said Squidward, and he went
back to sleep.

The next morning a very annoyed
Squidward and sleepy Patrick
headed over to Sandy's treedome.
"What are we going to do about
SpongeBob?" asked Squidward.
"I refuse to be ordered around
by him anymore."

"I have just the thing
    for the little guy," said Sandy.

"To express our gratitude
for all your hard work, we have a
small present for you," said Sandy.
"For me?" asked SpongeBob.
SpongeBob opened the box.
Inside was a camp uniform.

"We would like you to be the very
first camper," said Sandy.
"But don't you need me to work?"
asked SpongeBob.
"Nope. We were all so busy preparing
for camp that we never advertised
for campers! You are our first
and only camper!" exclaimed Sandy.

SpongeBob put on his uniform.
"SpongeBob SquarePants
reporting to camp!" he shouted,
running to his counselors.
"I am ready!"

THE BIG WIN

by Kelli Chipponeri
illustrated by Dave Aikins

The Bikini Bottom Relay Race
was just three days away. It only
happened once every five years!
SpongeBob and his friends
could not wait to compete.

It was the first day of practice. SpongeBob, Patrick, Sandy, Gary, Mr. Krabs, and Squidward were each going to compete in an event. "Team," said Squidward. "We have to train hard if we are going to win the golden booty treasure chest. So I am going to coach you!"

"Good idea!" said SpongeBob.
"Gold, sweet gold!" said Mr. Krabs.

SpongeBob practiced
ship-mast pole vaulting.
He ran, stuck the mast in the sand,
and swung himself over the ship.
"Great job, buddy!" said Sandy.
But Squidward was not impressed.

Then Patrick practiced
the sailing long jump.
He ran, flaring out his arms
and legs to jump far.
"Jump farther!" called Squidward.

Sandy and Mr. Krabs practiced their
events. Mr. Krabs spun around,
then tossed the sand-dollar discus.
Sandy ran and threw the javelin.
"Not good enough!" cried Squidward.
"What is it with you people!?"

Even Gary was going to compete!
He practiced hurdling coral.
"We are never going to win if
you move this slowly, Gary!"
cried Squidward, annoyed.

Then it was Squidward's turn.
He picked up a kelp log
and practiced tossing it.
"Nice throw, Squidward!"
his teammates cheered.

"Team meeting!" called Squidward.

The team jogged over happily.

"Great practice!" cheered Sandy.

"Am I sweaty?" SpongeBob asked.

"Let's do it again!" cried Patrick.

"Meow!" agreed Gary.

"Quiet!" said their coach.
"We will never win first place
 if we compete like that.
 Tomorrow we need to work harder!"
"Okay," said the team, unsure why.

They thought practice went well.

"We have to go for the gold!"

Squidward reminded them.

"Ah, sweet gold!" said Mr. Krabs.

The next day at practice
SpongeBob tried hard to vault high.
"HIGHER!" demanded Squidward.
"We must win that pirate's booty!"

Patrick strained to make his arms
and legs as long as possible.
"LONGER!" Squidward shouted.
"Think about the treasure chest!"

"Spin, Krabs!" cried Squidward.

"Throw it FARTHER, Sandy!"
barked Squidward. "Go for the gold!"

"Faster, Gary! FASTER!"

But Gary still moved too slowly.

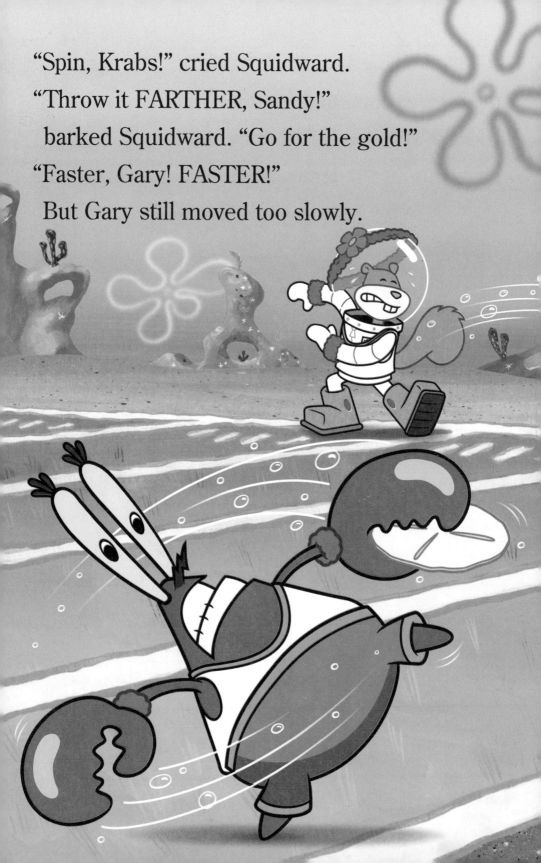

"Who am I kidding? We can't win.
I might as well just go home and
hang my head in shame,"
said Squidward, kicking the grass.

TWEET! Squidward blew his whistle.
"Okay people. My mother always says
if I want something done right,
I have to do it myself," he said.

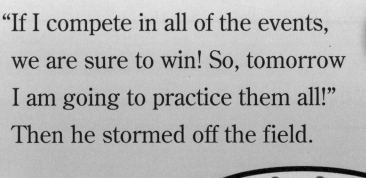

"If I compete in all of the events, we are sure to win! So, tomorrow I am going to practice them all!" Then he stormed off the field.

"Squidward wants to win so badly that he is making us miserable," Sandy told the rest of the gang.

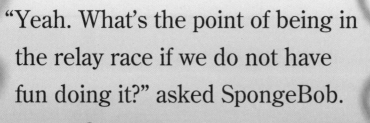

"Yeah. What's the point of being in the relay race if we do not have fun doing it?" asked SpongeBob.

The next day Squidward practiced
all of his teammates' events.

When it was time for his event,
Squidward was so tired he could
barely throw the log.

"Squidward," Sandy said. "You can't compete in everything. You should trust that we will do our best."

"What if we do not win?" he asked.

"What, no gold?" cried Mr. Krabs.

"Winning isn't everything," Sandy said.
"Stop worrying about winning and enjoy
  being teammates with us!"
"Yeah!" agreed the group.
"Not compete just to win?" he said.
"Mmm, I guess we could try it."

The day of the race the team was warming up, when *TWEET! TWEET!* "Team meeting!" called Squidward. The team huddled. "Just do your best!" Squidward said. "Go team!" they cheered.

"Fly, SpongeBob, fly!"
cheered Squidward.
"Jump, Patrick, jump!
"Throw, Sandy, throw!"
coached Squidward.
"Spin, Krabs baby, spin!"

59

"Hurdle, Gary, hurdle!" cheered Squidward, as Gary trailed behind the other hurdlers.

Squidward picked up the
kelp log and let it go.
The log flew through the air.
"Go, Squidward!" cheered his team.

"Second place," sighed Squidward.
"True, we didn't win the gold,"
said SpongeBob. "But we worked
well together and had fun! We could
have come in third."

"Of course," replied Squidward,
"if you weren't such slugs,
we could have won, but . . ."
"SLUGS!" the team cried.
Squidward smiled. "I mean
slugs in the kindest way."

Squidward's teammates were right.
They did have a good time. And that
made them all feel like winners!